The Summer Maker

an ojibway indian myth

Retold by Margery Bernstein and Janet Kobrin
Illustrated by Anne Burgess

CHARLES SCRIBNER'S SONS, NEW YORK

Text copyright © 1977 Margery Bernstein and Janet Kobrin
Illustrations copyright © 1977 Anne Burgess

Library of Congress Cataloging in Publication Data

Bernstein, Margery.
The summer maker.
SUMMARY: An easy-to-read retelling of the Ojibway
Indian myth about the creation of summer.
1. Chippewa Indians—Legends. 2. Indians of North
America—Legends. [1. Chippewa Indians—Legends.
2. Indians of North America—Legends] I. Kobrin,
Janet, joint author. II. Burgess, Anne, 1942-
III. Title.
E99.C6I 67   398.2 36   [398.2]   76-14875
ISBN 0-684-14716-5

1 3 5 7 9 11 13 15 17 19 MD/C 20 18 16 14 12 10 8 6 4 2

Printed in the United States of America

c.4

To
Edgar Bernstein
and
Philip Montag

whose talents created the Independent
Learning Project, and whose support and
enthusiasm made this book possible.

Once, long ago, there was only winter in the world. It was always cold, and the snow never melted.

The animals were used to winter. They had never known anything else. But in the stories from long ago they had heard about something called Summer. The old stories told of a time when the winds were warm and the earth was green.

In that wintry time, a fisher named Ojeeg lived on the shores of an icy lake.

Ojeeg did not mind the cold and snow. He had a fur coat to keep him warm. He was a good hunter, and always brought home plenty of food for his wife and son.

Ojeeg's son wanted to be a great hunter like his father, but he was not big and strong. When he came home from hunting each day he was shivering and covered with snow. He never caught anything.

One night when Ojeeg came home, his son began to cry.

"What's wrong?" asked his father.

"I am crying because I am always cold," answered the son. "I am crying because the snow is too deep and I can't hunt."

Ojeeg wanted to help his son. "I have heard stories about something long ago called Summer. It was warm then and there was no snow," Ojeeg said. "The old stories tell about a land above the mountains. Maybe we can find Summer there."

Then Ojeeg called his friends together.
Otter, Beaver, Lynx, and Wolverine listened
while he told them of a time without
snow and cold. He asked if they would go
with him to find Summer.

Otter did not stop to think. He
answered quickly.

"I will go," he said. "I am strong and
fast. I am so clever that it will be easy for
me to find Summer."

Beaver and Lynx and Wolverine
thought about it for a while. Then they
said, "We will go too. But it will be more
difficult than you think!"

So Ojeeg and his friends started for the high mountains. Otter sang and danced and talked as they went along.

The animals walked and walked for many days. Otter stopped singing and dancing and started to complain.

"I am tired of walking," he said. "This is no fun. Why don't we go home?"

The others did not answer him. They
just walked on and on through the forests
and across the plains.

At last they came to the high
mountains.

"What do we do now?" Beaver asked.
"Where do we go?"

"Let's go home," said Otter.

"We must climb the mountains," said
Ojeeg. "Perhaps we can find someone to
help us on the way."

So they began to climb.

When they were halfway up the mountain they saw a small lodge.

"Maybe someone here can tell us where to find Summer," said Lynx.

They all hurried toward the lodge—all except Otter, who stopped and pointed. He pointed at a huge creature which was standing in the doorway.

The animals had never before seen anything like it. It looked so funny to them that they all began to laugh.

But Ojeeg said, "Do not laugh! I have heard of creatures like this. It is a powerful spirit called a manitou. We must be very careful not to make it angry. It may know where to find Summer, but if we laugh at the manitou it won't help us."

The manitou waved to the animals and invited them into its lodge. While they warmed themselves near the fire, the manitou gave them food and water.

While they ate, the animals looked closely at the manitou. It looked even funnier than before. It was hard for them not to laugh, but everyone kept quiet— everyone except for Otter. He began to laugh softly.

"What is that noise?" asked the manitou angrily.

"My friend Otter has a cold," answered Ojeeg. "He was just sneezing."

Ojeeg sat down beside Otter. "Stop that!" he whispered.

Otter laughed again.

"What was that noise?" asked the manitou. It was even angrier than before.

"My friend just blew his nose," Ojeeg answered quickly.

"You had better stop or we will have to sit on you," Ojeeg warned Otter softly.

But Otter laughed again.

"What was that noise?" roared the manitou. "It sounds like laughter! If I hear it again you must leave!"

Ojeeg, Beaver, Wolverine, and Lynx all sat on Otter's head!

Otter did not laugh again.

When the animals were ready to leave, they asked the manitou if it knew where to find Summer.

The manitou knew where to go and what to do. It told them how to bring Summer to the world.

Ojeeg and his friends did what the manitou told them. They climbed to the very top of the mountain. They sat down and began to smoke their pipes.

As the smoke rose from their pipes, they suddenly saw a crack in the bottom of the sky. The crack was right over their heads.

"There it is!" cried Ojeeg. "The manitou told us the crack would be here. It said if we could use the crack to break the sky open we would find Summer in the land above.

"Who wants to break open the bottom of the sky?"

"I'll do it," said Otter. "It's easy!"

Otter jumped up against the sky. He made a loud thump, but nothing happened.

"We'll never break it open," said Otter. "Let's go home."

"Wait," said Beaver quietly.
"Let me try."

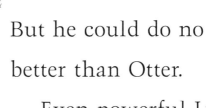

But he could do no
better than Otter.
Even powerful Lynx
could not widen the crack.
Then they all turned
to Wolverine.

"You are the only one left," said Ojeeg. "If you cannot break a hole in the bottom of the sky, we must go home without Summer."

"I will try my best," said Wolverine.

The first time
Wolverine jumped,
nothing happened.

The second time,
the crack got bigger.

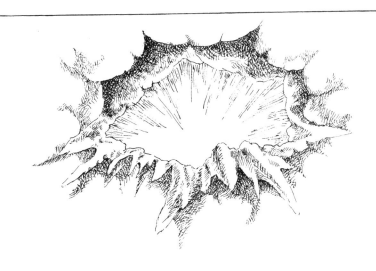

The third time, with a loud noise,
Wolverine split the bottom of the sky!

Quickly the animals jumped through the hole onto the land above. They were very surprised!

The world above was warm! There was no snow! There was no cold wind!

Here the land was green. They had found Summer.

The animals looked and saw many
lodges under the big green trees. Ojeeg
and his friends saw no people, but in the
lodges there were many cages filled with
beautiful birds.

"We must do what the manitou told us," Ojeeg said. "Let these birds out of their cages! Do it quietly and quickly. We must be finished and gone before the people who keep the birds come back."

Silently, the animals ran from lodge to lodge. They opened all the cages.

Hundreds of birds poured out. They flew up into the air and then down through the hole in the bottom of the sky— down to the world below. The warm winds followed the birds. The snow began to melt on earth, and the trees began to turn green.

The animals were almost finished opening all the cages, but Otter could not keep still.

"Look, look, my friends!" he shouted. "We have done it! We have let Summer into the world!"

The Bird Keepers heard Otter shouting. They came running from the woods to see what had happened. First they saw their birds flying away. Then they saw Ojeeg and his friends. "Catch them!" the Bird Keepers screamed. "They have let Summer out! Catch them!"

The Bird Keepers began to chase Ojeeg and his friends. The animals were frightened. They ran back toward the hole as fast as they could.

Otter was the first to jump through the hole. Beaver was next, and then Lynx, and finally Wolverine. They were so frightened that they ran all the way down the mountain without ever looking back.

Only Ojeeg did not reach the hole!

The Bird Keepers had chased him toward the woods, and he was running so fast and so hard that he could not stop. He dashed up a tree and scrambled all the way to the top of the sky. There, he clung to the stars.

Ojeeg looked around and saw that there was no way for him to get back down. The tops of the tallest trees were far below him. He could never reach the earth again.

But Ojeeg discovered that he could look down and see everything that was happening in the world. He watched his family and friends at home. He saw his son grow up and become a great hunter.

And every year Ojeeg watched the birds come flying in with the warm winds to melt the snow and bring Summer. He was content.